Rabbit
COLORING BOOK!

DISCOVER THIS UNIQUE
COLLECTION OF COLORING PAGES

Bold Illustrations
COLORING BOOKS

This is a Bleed Through Page If You Are Using a Colouring Marker or Pen!

Find Other Great Titles By searching for Bold Illustrations on Your Favorite Book Retailer

Amazon.Ca | Barnes & Noble (BN.Com) | Books A Million (BAM.Com)

Bold Illustrations

COLORING BOOKS

This is a Bleed Through Page If You Are Using a Colouring Marker or Pen!
Find Other Great Titles By searching for Bold Illustrations on Your Favorite Book Retailer
Amazon.Ca | Barnes & Noble (BN.Com) | Books A Million (BAM.Com)

Bold Illustrations
COLORING BOOKS

This is a Bleed Through Page If You Are Using a Colouring Marker or Pen!

Find Other Great Titles By searching for Bold Illustrations on Your Favorite Book Retailer

Amazon.Ca | Barnes & Noble (BN.Com) | Books A Million (BAM.Com)

Bold Illustrations

COLORING BOOKS

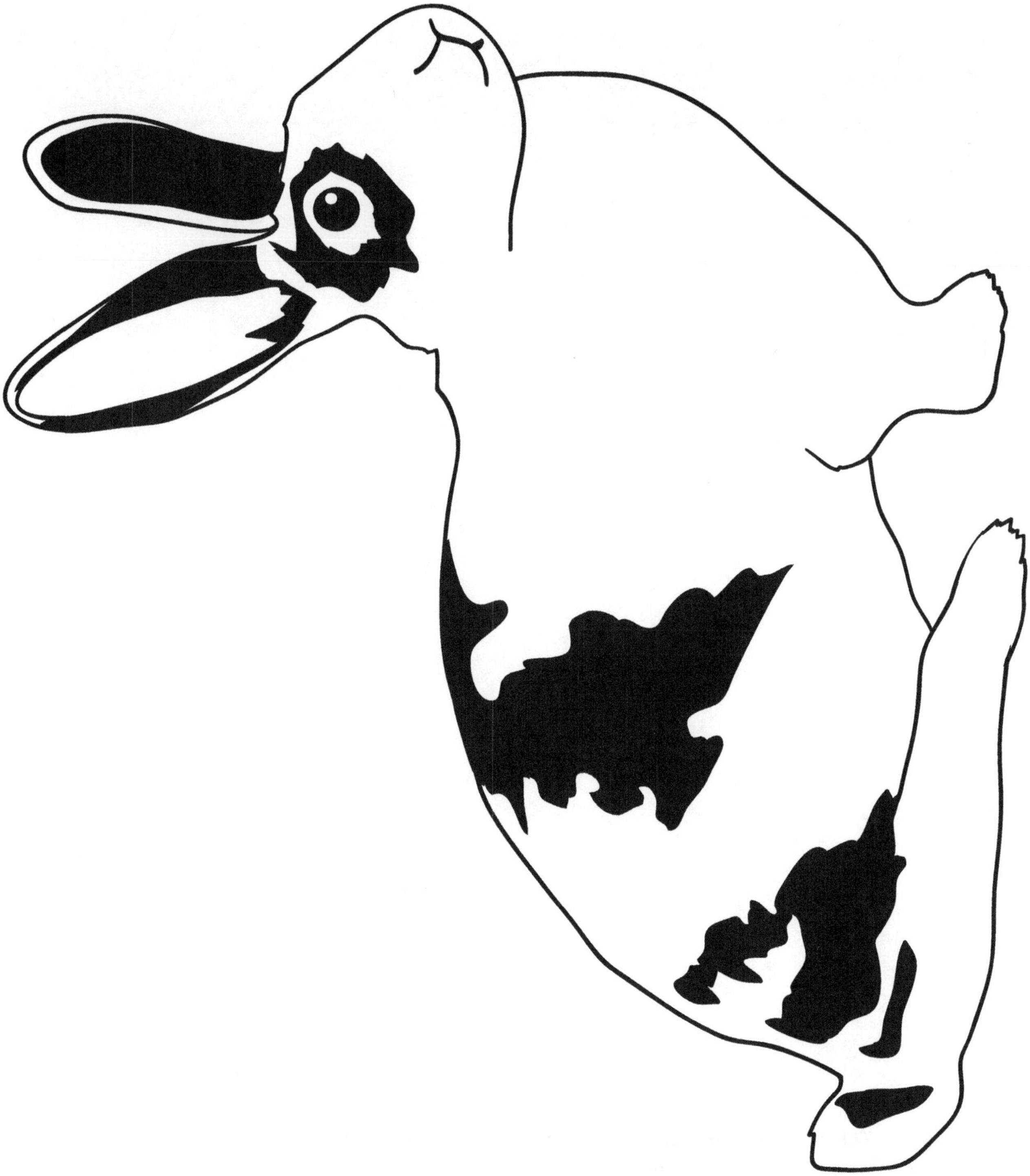

This is a Bleed Through Page If You Are Using a Colouring Marker or Pen!

Find Other Great Titles By searching for Bold Illustrations on Your Favorite Book Retailer

Amazon.Ca | Barnes & Noble (BN.Com) | Books A Million (BAM.Com)

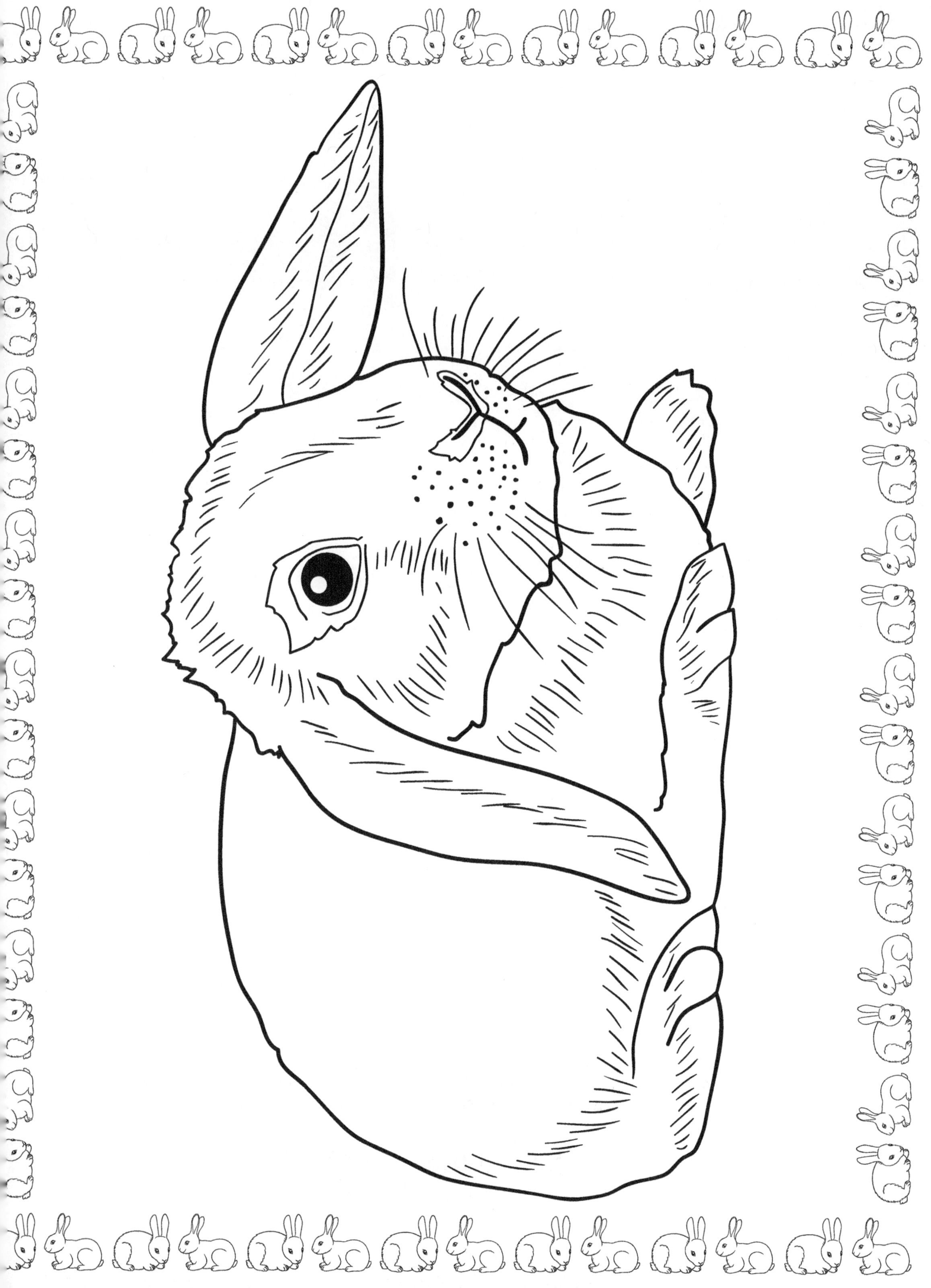

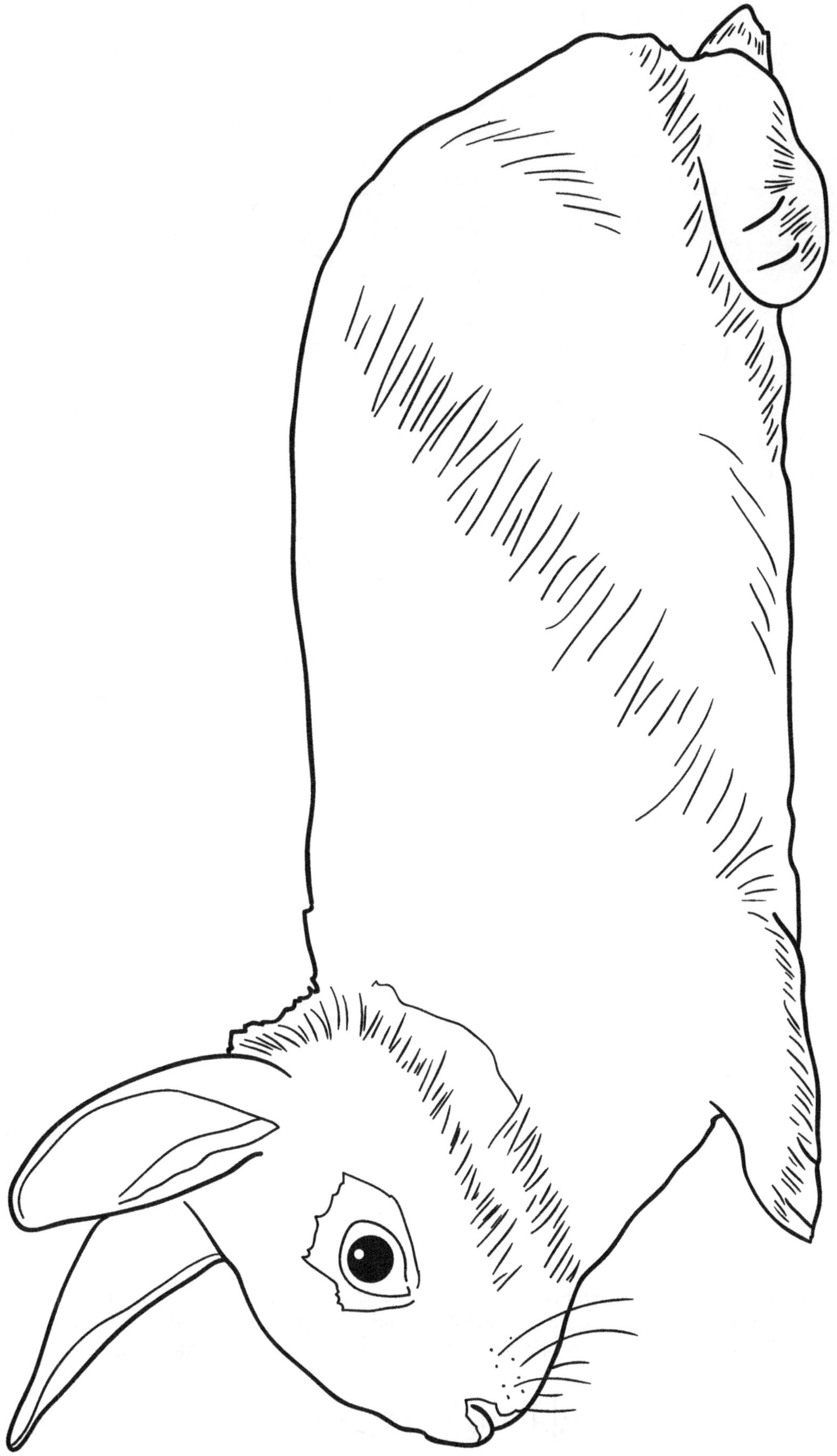

This is a Bleed Through Page If You Are Using a Colouring Marker or Pen!

Find Other Great Titles By searching for Bold Illustrations on Your Favorite Book Retailer

Amazon.Ca | Barnes & Noble (BN.Com) | Books A Million (BAM.Com)

Made in the USA
Monee, IL
16 May 2022